MW01595307

learn from water beauts!
The life force that will
help us Survive

Water

4/9/15

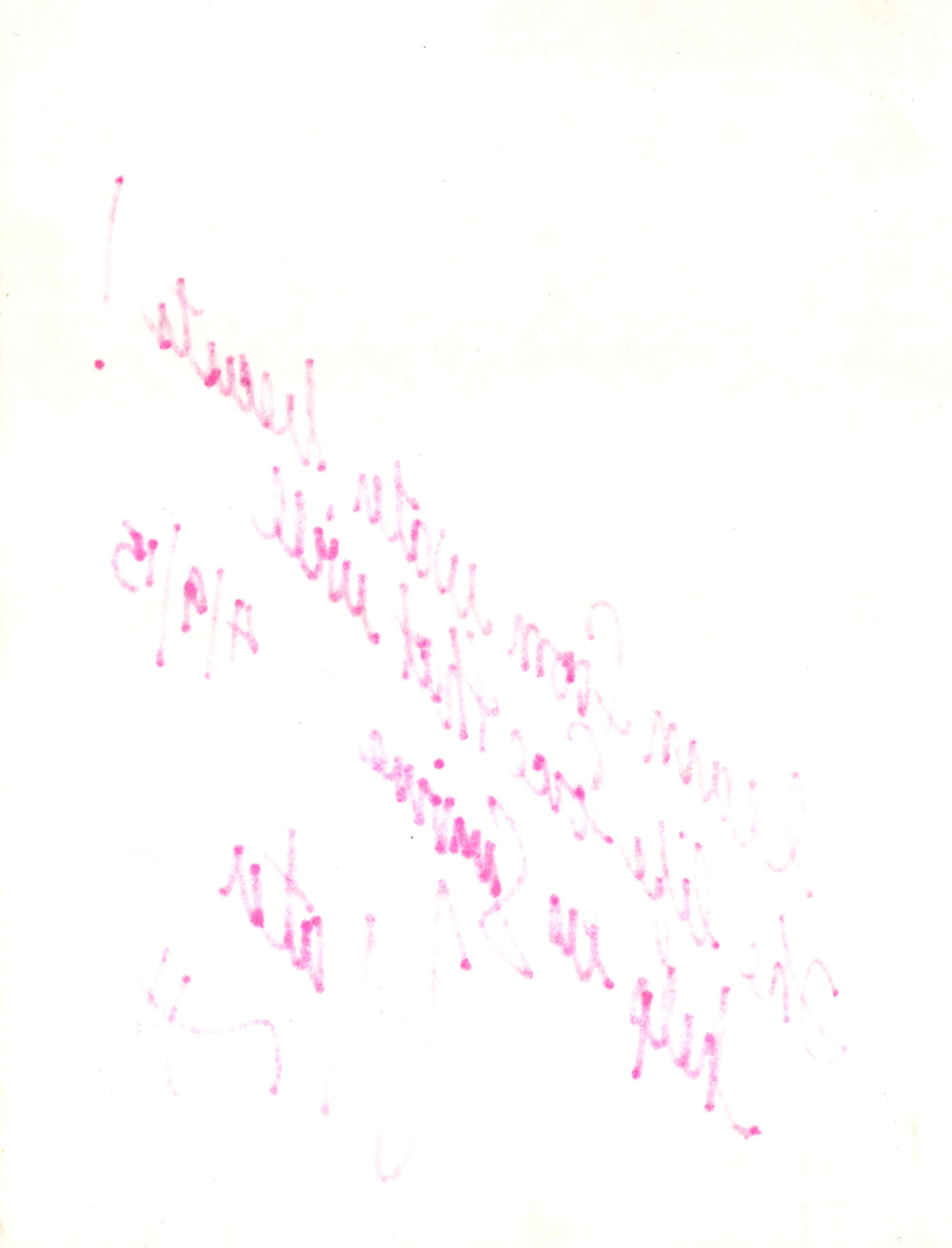

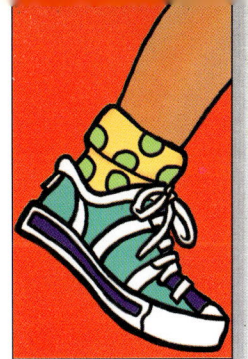

First Sports Science

In the
Water

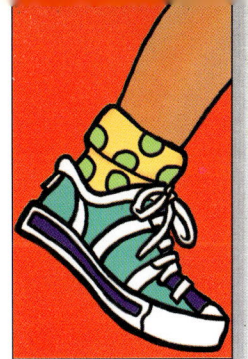

Nikki Bundey

Carolrhoda Books, Inc. Minneapolis

All words that appear in **bold** are explained in Words We Use, which begins on page 30.

Photographs courtesy of:

Vince Cavataio 24b / Allsport; Tom Nebbia 29 / 8t / Aspect Picture Library; I.Z.Dawson 13b, 15, 17t, 18b, 19t / DDA Photo Library; Bruce Stephens - cover (inset, tr), 10b, 11, 26 / Peter Arkell 12 / Maria Pawel 14t / Impact Photos; Anthony Bannister 14b / Norbert Wu 22b / NHPA; 20t / Philip Sauvain Picture Collection; David Callow 10t / 16t, 17b / Sporting Pictures (U.K.); J.Frebet 8b / Still Pictures; Marco Polo 28b / Telegraph Colour Library; cover (background), title page, 4t & b, 5, 9, 13t, 16b, 18t, 19b, 20b, 21, 22t, 23, 24t, 25, 27b, 28t / Zefa.

Illustrations by Virginia Gray

This edition first published in the United States in 1998 by Carolrhoda Books, Inc.

A ZOË BOOK

Copyright © 1997 by Zoë Books Limited. First published in 1997 by Zoë Books Limited, Winchester, England.

Carolrhoda Books, Inc. c/o The Lerner Publishing Group
241 First Avenue North, Minneapolis, MN 55401 U.S.A.

Library of Congress Cataloging-in-Publication Data

Bundey, Nikki.
    In the water / Nikki Bundey; [illustrations by Virginia Gray].
      p. cm. — (First sports science)
    Includes index.
    Summary: Presents some basic information about such concepts of physics as energy, bouyance, and waves while describing the mechanics of various water sports, including swimming, surfing, and boating.
    ISBN 1–57505–085–4 (alk. paper)
      1. Aquatic sports — Juvenile literature. 2. Physics. — Study and teaching
  — Juvenile literature. [1. Aquatic sports. 2. Physics.]
  I. Gray, Virginia, ill. II. Title. III. Series.
  GV770.5.B85 1998
  797 — dc21   96-40012

Printed in Italy by Grafedit SpA
Bound in the United States of America

1 2 3 4 5 6 02 01 00 99 98 97

Contents

Making a Splash 4

Get Fit! 6

Fuel for the Body 8

Safety First! 10

Floating 12

Learning to Swim 14

Swimming Skills 16

Jumping and Diving 18

Dressed to Swim 20

Underwater Survival 22

Skimming the Surface 24

Paddling and Rowing 26

Wind Power 28

Words we Use 30

Index 32

All the words that appear in **bold** are explained in Words we use on page 30.

4

Making a Splash

Water falls to the Earth as rain or snow. The rain fills streams and rivers, lakes and seas. Oceans of salt water cover two-thirds of the Earth's surface. People pipe water into towns and homes for drinking, washing, and even swimming.

This child is swimming under water. The water flows around her body. The movement of her body causes splashes and ripples on the water's surface.

Slides and chutes are lots of fun at the pool. Water makes the slide's surface slippery, so you go down faster.

What is water like? It is a clear liquid that flows and swirls and splashes and bubbles. It feels wet and makes things slippery.

Most people love playing with water. Many sports take place in or under the water. We swim and dive. We play games such as water polo. Other sports, such as canoeing, surfing, and waterskiing, take place on the surface of the water.

Water polo is a team game. There are seven players on each side. The ball is passed between them. The aim is to score the most goals.

Get Fit!

Water sports are good for us.
Exercise makes us take air into our
lungs. The lungs pass **oxygen**,
which we need to live, into the
blood. Exercise also helps our hearts
to pump blood around our bodies.

Water sports such as swimming and
surfing help to build up our
arm and leg muscles.
These sports help
make us fit.

Water sports
make our
bodies work
hard.

The lungs pass
oxygen
into the blood.

The heart pumps
blood full of oxygen
around the body.

Blood vessels are
tubes that carry
blood to every
part of the body.

The power to move is called **energy**. Water weighs more than air, so we need more energy to move through water than through air. Swimming can be hard work. It uses a lot of energy.

Some water sports are not such hard work. We just enjoy them, and that's good for us too.

Which parts of the body do you think swimming helps to make strong?

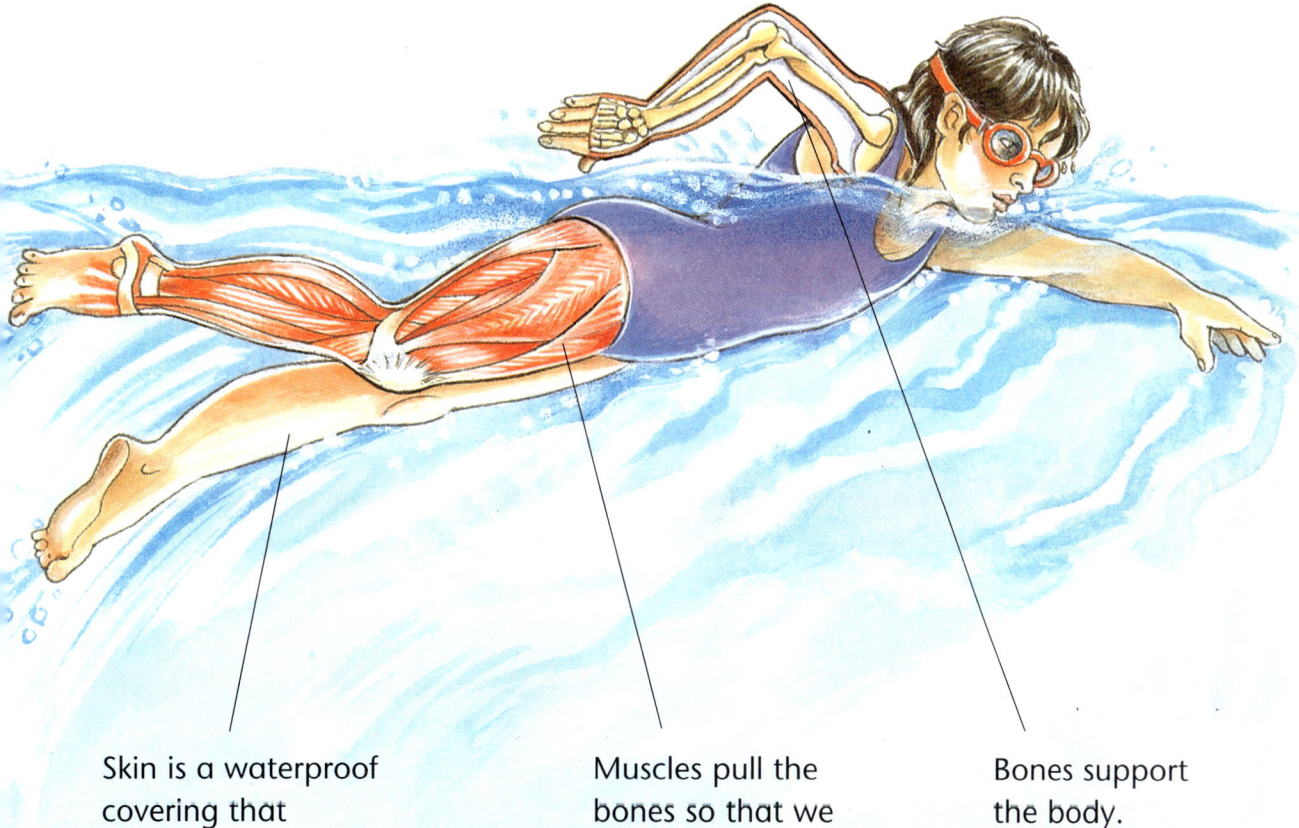

Skin is a waterproof covering that protects the body.

Muscles pull the bones so that we can move.

Bones support the body.

8

Fuel for the Body

Our bodies need fuel to work well. Just as cars need gas and oil, we need food and water.

We take water into our bodies by drinking and by eating foods that contain it, such as fruit and vegetables. So water isn't just fun to play in – it is also a fuel that keeps us alive.

Having a picnic on the beach is fun. But your body needs time to digest the food. Do not go swimming too soon after you have eaten a meal.

The water we drink must be fresh and clean. We cannot drink salty seawater or water that is dirty or full of chemicals.

Our bodies need the right amount of fuel. Too much food and drink makes us too heavy, or overweight. Too little food leaves us weak or ill. We also need the right mixture of foods to stay healthy. This is called a balanced diet.

What foods and drinks do you like? Are they good for you? Try not to eat too many fatty and sweet foods. Eat plenty of fresh vegetables and fruits, bread, and milk. A balanced diet helps to keep you fit.

Safety First!

Humans can hold their breath underwater. But unlike fish, we cannot breathe by taking oxygen from the water. We need to take oxygen from the air. If we are underwater for too long without air, we will drown. Water sports are fun but they can be dangerous. Follow the safety rules carefully. The better you can swim, the safer you will be. Don't risk drowning.

These lifeguards are showing how to save the life of a surfer or swimmer who gets into difficulty. One of them breathes air into the lungs.

Always wear a life jacket for sports such as canoeing or sailing. It will keep you afloat if you fall into the water.

Here are some safety rules.

- Always make sure a grown-up is nearby and knows what you are doing.

- Don't go into deep water unless you are a skilled swimmer.

- Learn the correct way of doing things. Never go canoeing or boating without training.

- Beware of strong **currents** and bad weather. Obey any warning flags or notices.

- Look before you jump or dive. Make sure the water is deep enough.

- Always wear life jackets for surface sports.

- Know what to do in an emergency. Know how to use a telephone and get help.

- Cover bare skin with **sunblock**. Too much sun can harm the skin and make you sick.

Life buoys are used to rescue people who fall in. The buoys are thrown into the water. People can grab hold of them to stay afloat.

Floating

Things that are light or full of air will float in water. Things that are heavy will sink. Boats and ships are full of air, so they float even when they are very heavy. They are helped by a force called **buoyancy**. The bottom of the boat pushes down into the water, but the water pushes up and keeps the boat afloat.

The buoyancy of water supports the body. This helps people with muscle or movement problems to exercise in water.

Hold on to a kickboard. Kick with your legs and move forward through the water. Get used to the feeling of buoyancy.

Many small children use armbands when they learn to swim. These are filled with air to help the children to stay afloat. Later, children may hold on to kickboards. Soon they find they can stay afloat without help.

The air in your lungs and the buoyancy of the water will hold you up. You can float on your back or on your front.

Learning to Swim

At first, water may seem wet, cold, and nasty. But once you're in, it's fun. Keep moving to stay warm.

Walking through air is easy. Walking on the bottom of a swimming pool is much harder. The water presses against the whole of your body. It could be worse –

To swim safely and well, you learn the best way to move through the water.

Frogs are powerful swimmers. Their strong legs push them through the water. Try kicking out and stretching like a frog.

imagine wading through a swimming pool filled with jelly!

If your body is stretched out flat, or horizontal, it will slip through water easily. To swim quickly, you need to make a **streamlined** shape like a fish. Which parts of your body do you use to move yourself forward? Which parts do you use for steering?

Many people first swim by kicking and pulling at the water. This is sometimes called the dog paddle, because it is the way dogs swim.

Swimming Skills

There are different ways of moving through the water. These are called swimming strokes. Each stroke has its own arm and leg movements. You have to learn the best time to take a breath – without swallowing water! And you should learn how to make a turn when you have finished a width or length of the pool.

Overarm movements make the **crawl** powerful and fast. The legs kick up and down. The head is low in the water.

The **backstroke** is like an upside-down crawl. You lie on your back and kick yourself forward. Your arms circle backward. Be careful – you won't be able to see where you are going!

The **breaststroke** is relaxing. Swim on your front and push yourself forward with froglike kicks. Push both arms forward. Stretch them out, around, and back to the chest.

Which of these strokes do you think is the most tiring? Which is the steadiest and smoothest? Which stroke might you use if you had to swim to the shore through stormy seas?

You have to be very fit to do the **butterfly**. Both arms come forward to scoop the water at once. Your chest lifts out of the water.

Jumping and Diving

Jumping in is fun. But look before you leap! Then hold your breath and go. Does your body travel faster through the air or through the water? At what point does it slow down? Why does it bob back to the surface?

Hold your body upright, or vertical, as you jump in. If you enter the pool at an angle, more of your body will hit the water. You will make a bigger splash, but you may hurt yourself.

You can start learning to dive by sitting on the edge of the pool. Hold your breath. Point your arms forward, tuck your head down, and topple in headfirst. Glide back to the surface.

To dive from a standing position, point your arms and then jump up to gain height. Bend your body forward so that you enter the water vertically, not flat on your stomach. Belly flops can be dangerous, and they hurt.

Once you have dived from the side of a pool, you might try diving from a bouncy **springboard**. This helps you to gain height so that you enter the water at the best possible angle. Be careful not to slip and hit the board.

High boards are scary! You must learn how to dive from a height.

Experienced divers do not splash much as they enter water. Some divers can do somersaults and other moves in midair.

Dressed to Swim

One hundred years ago, men swam in long, woolly vests and pants. Women wore frilly bathing costumes and caps.

Modern swimsuits are close-fitting and waterproof. They are streamlined so water flows around the swimmer without too much contact to slow the swimmer down. Some swimmers wear bathing caps to be even more streamlined.

This is what a fashionable young lady wore for swimming in France in the 1880s. Compare her ribbons and frills with a modern swimsuit.

Modern swimwear does not get in the way when you are swimming fast. It is made of artificial fibers.

Wet suits are made of a rubberlike material called neoprene. They are usually lined with nylon and fit snugly around the body. Surfers and divers wear them.

Wet suits keep you warm in cold seas. Why is this important? What might happen if you got too cold?

Wet suits make it possible to swim in cold seas, even in winter. They also protect the body against cuts from underwater rocks.

Underwater Survival

Swimming underwater is fun. For short periods, you can hold your breath underwater. A **snorkel** helps you to take air from the surface through a short pipe held in your mouth. Snorkels are used for exploring rockpools and reefs but cannot be used for deep-sea diving.

Flippers add force to your kick. They are like the webbed feet of some water animals.

These tourists in Florida are snorkeling over a coral reef. Snorkelers can often see wonderful sea creatures and shells.

The flipper design of this sea lion's feet makes it a good swimmer. Divers wear rubber flippers. These are bigger and bend more than our feet. They push back more water and make us move faster.

During long, deep dives, people need their own supply of air to breathe. They carry air tanks on their backs. This equipment is called **scuba**, standing for **s**elf-**c**ontained **u**nderwater **b**reathing **a**pparatus. Scuba diving is an exciting sport for strong, experienced swimmers.

This scuba diver has met a white-tip reef shark off Hawaii. Air that the swimmer has breathed out forms bubbles that rise to the surface.

Skimming the Surface

Water presses against objects and holds them back. The less contact objects have with the water, the faster they can move. Water skis skim across the water's surface at high speed, with very little contact. Water-skiers grip a line towed by a boat. Some water-skiers have reached speeds of up to 100 miles per hour.

The water-skier leans and angles the skis to move from side to side.

The size of waves depends on the wind, the shape of the seabed, and ocean currents. The depth of most waves is about half the **wavelength**, which is the distance from one crest to another.

Surfers move with the power of the waves. They hold on to floats and boards that carry them forward.

Experienced surfers stand on their surfboards. They control their feet, legs, and arms to find perfect balance. Surfers must beware of dangerous currents.

Surfers can ride waves up to about 30 feet high in Hawaii. Surfboards are made from hardened plastic foam and have a streamlined design.

Paddling and Rowing

When we swim, we push our bodies forward with our arms and hands. We can push a canoe forward with paddles. The paddles are longer, stiffer, and wider than our arms and hands. They push against more water with greater force, so the canoe goes faster.

Canoes are shallow and long with pointed ends. They can overturn easily.

Canoeists wear life jackets and helmets for safety. Canoes are made of lightweight materials so they will float easily.

oars push against the water

boat moves forward

The rower uses the oars to push the rowboat forward. The oars can steer the boat as well. Pushing the water in one direction turns the boat in the other direction.

Oars are used in rowboats. They are placed in holders called **oarlocks**. This means that the oars work better as **levers** as they push the boat forwards. Rowboats are bigger and heavier than canoes.

You can learn to row on any boating pond. When you are older, you may learn to race light boats at high speed. This is called **sculling**.

Wind Power

Muscles, motors, and oars can all push us through or over the water. Sails push boards and boats over the surface by catching the wind.

Sailboarding, or windsurfing, brings together the fun of surfing and the skills of sailing. Hang on and keep your balance! The board can skim forward at more than 40 miles per hour.

Wind, balance, and body position can make the sailboard leap from the water.

You may start off dry and warm, but be prepared to get wet! Sailboards overturn more easily than boats, so always follow the safety rules.

Sailing boats may be small **dinghies** or ocean-going **yachts**. Their **hulls** must be tough. What might happen if they sprang a leak?

Sails are usually made of strong artificial fibers. Sailors steer to make the best use of the wind. Sometimes they must **tack** to do this.

These young people are learning to sail on a tall ship. They learn to climb the **rigging** and hoist the sails. Two hundred years ago, all big ships were powered by sail.

Words We Use

backstroke: swimming on your back by moving the arms backward over the head

breaststroke: a swimming stroke in which the arms thrust forward and then curve back. The legs do a frog kick.

buoyancy: a force that keeps things afloat

butterfly: a swimming stroke in which both arms are flung forwards at the same time

crawl: an overarm swimming stroke

current: a rapid movement of water in part of a river or sea

dinghy: a small, open boat that has oars or paddles. Dinghies often have sails.

hull: the shell-like body or frame of a boat or ship

lever: a bar that is held or rested on something so that when one end is moved, the other moves in the opposite direction

oarlock: a support for an oar on the side of a boat

oxygen: a gas, found in air and water, that all animals need to live

rigging: the ropes that work masts and sails

sailboarding: using a board fitted with a simple sail to skim over the water. Also called windsurfing.

scuba: a system of air tanks and tubes that allows divers to breathe underwater

sculling: racing lightweight rowboats using oars called sculls

snorkel: an air tube that is held in the mouth by an underwater swimmer and reaches above the water's surface, allowing the swimmer to breathe

springboard: a springy plank attached to the side of a pool for diving

streamlined: shaped to move through air or water easily, with little contact

sunblock: a cream or lotion that protects the skin by blocking out some of the sun's dangerous rays

tack: to steer a zigzag course to catch the wind

wavelength: the distance between the crest of one wave and the crest of the next

yacht: a sailing boat for pleasure or racing. Some yachts have engines too.

Index

bathing caps, 20
boating, 11, 27, 28, 29
breathing, 10, 16, 18, 22, 23
buoyancy, 12, 13

canoeing, 5, 11, 26, 27

diet, 8, 9
diving, 5, 11, 19, 21
drinking water, 4, 8

energy, 7

floating, 12, 13

levers, 27

muscles, 6, 7, 12, 28

oars, 27, 28
oxygen, 6, 10

rowing, 27

sailboarding, 28
sailing, 28, 29
scuba, 23
snorkeling, 22
streamlining, 15, 20
surfing, 5, 21, 25, 28
swimming strokes, 16, 17
swimming, 4, 5, 7, 10, 11, 14,
    15, 16, 20, 22, 26
swimsuits, 20

water safety, 10, 11
water, 4, 5, 7, 8, 12, 14, 16, 18,
    22, 24, 26
waterskiing, 5, 24
waves, 24
wing, 28